To my parents, Keith and Bertha,
for giving me the gift of reading.

Parent's Introduction

We Both Read is the first series of books designed to invite parents and children to share the reading of a story by taking turns reading aloud. This "shared reading" innovation, which was developed in conjunction with early reading specialists, invites parents to read the more sophisticated text on the left-hand pages, while children are encouraged to read the right-hand pages, which have been written at one of three early reading levels.

Reading aloud is one of the most important activities parents can share with their child to assist their reading development. However, *We Both Read* goes beyond reading *to* a child and allows parents to share reading *with* a child. *We Both Read* is so powerful and effective because it combines two key elements in learning: "showing" (the parent reads) and "doing" (the child reads). The result is not only faster reading development for the child, but a much more enjoyable and enriching experience for both!

Most of the words used in the child's text should be familiar to them. Others can easily be sounded out. An occasional difficult word will be first introduced in the parent's text, distinguished with **bold lettering**. Pointing out these words, as you read them, will help familiarize them to your child. You may also find it helpful to read the entire book aloud yourself the first time, then invite your child to participate on the second reading. Also note that the parent's text is preceded by a "talking parent" icon: ⌒ ; and the child's text is preceded by a "talking child" icon: ☺ .

We Both Read books is a fun, easy way to encourage and help your child to read — and a wonderful way to start your child off on a lifetime of reading enjoyment!

We Both Read: The New Red Bed

Text Copyright © 1999 by Sindy McKay
Illustrations Copyright © 1999 by Erin Marie Mauterer
All rights reserved

We Both Read™ is a trademark of Treasure Bay, Inc.

Published by Treasure Bay, Inc.
17 Parkgrove Drive
South San Francisco, CA 94080 USA

PRINTED IN SINGAPORE

Library of Congress Catalog Card Number: 98-61767

Hardcover ISBN: 1-891327-12-7
Paperback ISBN: 1-891327-16-X

FIRST EDITION

We Both Read® Books
Patent No. 5,957,693

WE BOTH READ™

The New
Red Bed

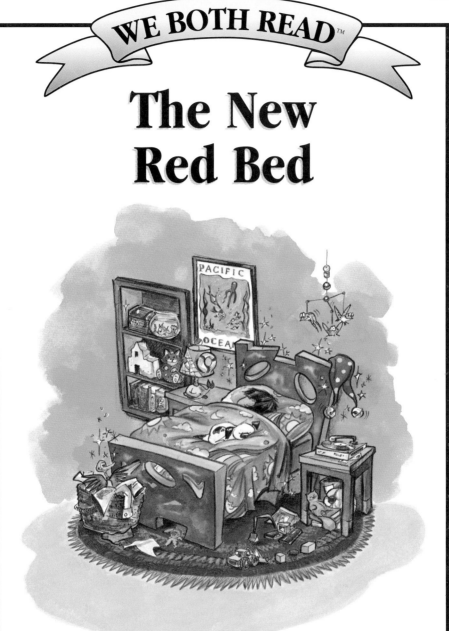

By Sindy McKay
Illustrated by Erin Marie Mauterer

TREASURE BAY

Last night at bedtime Sam's mom and dad said,
"Sam, we have a surprise for you."

Then off to his bedroom Sam was led.
And there he saw his new . . .

... red bed.

Sam jumped in the bed with his **dog**, named Ted, and closed his eyes up very tight.

Then he opened his eyes and looked through a fog. And on his red bed was his . . .

. . . **dog** on a frog.

Suddenly the frog leaped off of the bed. SPLASH — water splattered all over the place!

It splashed on **Sam**'s bed, and that was bad. His bed was brand new and . . .

. . . **Sam** was mad!

Sam followed the frog and Ted, his dog, and landed — head first — in a wonderful place!

For a place more remarkable Sam couldn't wish. Sam even saw some . . .

. . .fish on a dish.

Sam found Ted playing fetch with a fish.
"Come, Ted," Sam said. But the pup wouldn't budge.

So Sam began to **tug** on his pup.
He tried, but he just couldn't . . .

. . .**tug** the pup up.

Then Ted escaped with the help of his friend.
And Sam had to catch him all over again!

Sam **swam** over and grabbed his pup.
He held on tight and then . . .

. . .Sam **swam** up.

Sam and Ted finally reached the top. And all of a sudden the water was gone.

There were blankets and pillows and sheets instead. Sam was back . . .

. . . in his new red bed.

Sam closed his eyes and tried to sleep. But something was squirming down by his feet!

When he lifted the covers, he saw something big! He saw a big **pack**! Yes! . . .

. . . A big **pack** of pigs!

Sam said, "Hi," and the pigs said, "Hello."
They told Sam and Ted to join them below!

Sam crawled down to meet the Head Pig.
He said, "We are a pack of . . .

. . . pigs that dig!"

The pigs led Sam into a tunnel and Sam was amazed by what he saw there!

Sam saw these's and those's and this's and that's. He saw . . .

. . . green bats in hats
and big fat blue cats.

And that wasn't all that Sam saw there.
Wonderful things were everywhere!

Sam saw candy trees and marshmallow shrubs.
He saw . . .

. . . cows in cribs and . . .

. . . cubs in tubs.

Sam heard laughter and ran toward the sound.
He peeked in a cave—and guess what he found?

He found pigs that were laughing and dancing a jig.
But stranger than **that**, he found . . .

. . . pigs **that** had wigs!

They sang **rock** 'n' **roll**, and Sam joined in! Even
Ted danced along with a sweet Irish jig!

"What fun!" said the pigs. "Except when you trip!"
"I just love to . . .

". . . **rock**
and **roll**
and **rip!**"

Then the Head Pig said that the dancing was done. It was time for work — no more fun.

He told Sam to climb through the tunnel ahead. And soon Sam was back . . .

🪐 . . . in his new red bed.

Sam tried to sleep, but a noise woke him up. The noise was made by a **fly**ing duck!

The duck asked Sam, "Would you like to try to go up with me . . .

. . . and **fly** in the sky!"

Sam couldn't refuse an offer like that! So he spread out his arms and he started to flap!

He flapped and flapped and he flew right up. Then he looked down and saw . . .

. . . a pot of pink pups.

Sam was soaring above his bed! He was having great fun! And so was Ted!

From his perch up so high, Sam saw lots!
He saw . . .

. . . cups of cats with dots and spots!

Then Sam looked down on **six** trees below.
And there in one tree sat a large hippo!

She was building a nest made out of **sticks**.
She used . . .

. . . **six** stacks of **sticks**
and a big bag of bricks.

Ted chased the duck.   The duck was fine.
Sam was having a marvelous time!

Sam didn't want this night to be done.
Sam was having . . .

. . . too much fun!

 But, sooner or later, sleep has to come. So for Sam and Ted, tonight's fun is done.

Who knows what adventures still lie ahead for Sam and Ted in . . .

... the new red bed.

If you liked
The New Red Bed, **here are two other**
We Both Read™ **Books you are sure to enjoy!**

A very humorous updating of the classic story of three little pigs and a very bad wolf. With short and simple text for the very beginning reader, children will be delighted to participate in reading aloud this wonderful story.

Featuring the original illustrations of Beatrix Potter, this authorized adaptation retells the adventures of two little rabbits in Mr. McGregor's garden. In the first tale, Peter Rabbit disobeys his mother and goes into the garden, where he is almost caught by Mr. McGregor. In the second tale, he goes back with his cousin Benjamin. This time, Mr. McGregor may catch them both!